D1529509

THIS CANDLEWICK BOOK BELONGS TO:

_____

_____

_____

_____

*For Rita
and Brendan,
good friends*

M.W.

*For Paul,
Nick, and Emma,
my children*

J.B.

Text copyright © 1993 by Martin Waddell
Illustrations copyright © 1993 by Jill Barton

All rights reserved.

First U.S. paperback edition 1995

Library of Congress Cataloging-in-Publication Data

Waddell, Martin.
Little Mo / written by Martin Waddell ;
illustrated by Jill Barton.—1st U.S. ed.
Summary: The Big Ones try to help a young polar bear learn how
to glide on the ice, but she gets bumped so much that she decides
it isn't any fun—until she spends time learning on her own.
ISBN 1-56402-211-0 (hardcover) ISBN 1-56402-514-4 (paperback)
[1. Polar bear—Fiction.   2. Bears—Fiction.   3. Self-reliance—Fiction.]
I. Barton, Jill, ill.   II. Title.
PZ7.W1137Ll   1993
[E]—dc20   92-54410

10 9 8 7 6 5 4 3 2 1

Printed in Hong Kong

The pictures in this book were done in pencil and watercolor.

Candlewick Press
2067 Massachusetts Avenue
Cambridge, Massachusetts 02140

LITTLE
MO

Written by

Martin Waddell

Illustrated by

Jill Barton

CANDLEWICK PRESS
CAMBRIDGE, MASSACHUSETTS

Little Mo looked at the ice
and she liked it.

BUMP!

Little Mo got up   and tried sliding again.

BUMP!

A Big One came to help her.

More Big Ones came out onto the ice,

sliding and gliding around Little Mo.

They were her friends, all of them.

It was nice on the ice and she loved it.

The Big Ones whizzed and they whirled
and they twisted and twirled and
they raced and they jumped.

BUMP!   *BUMP!*

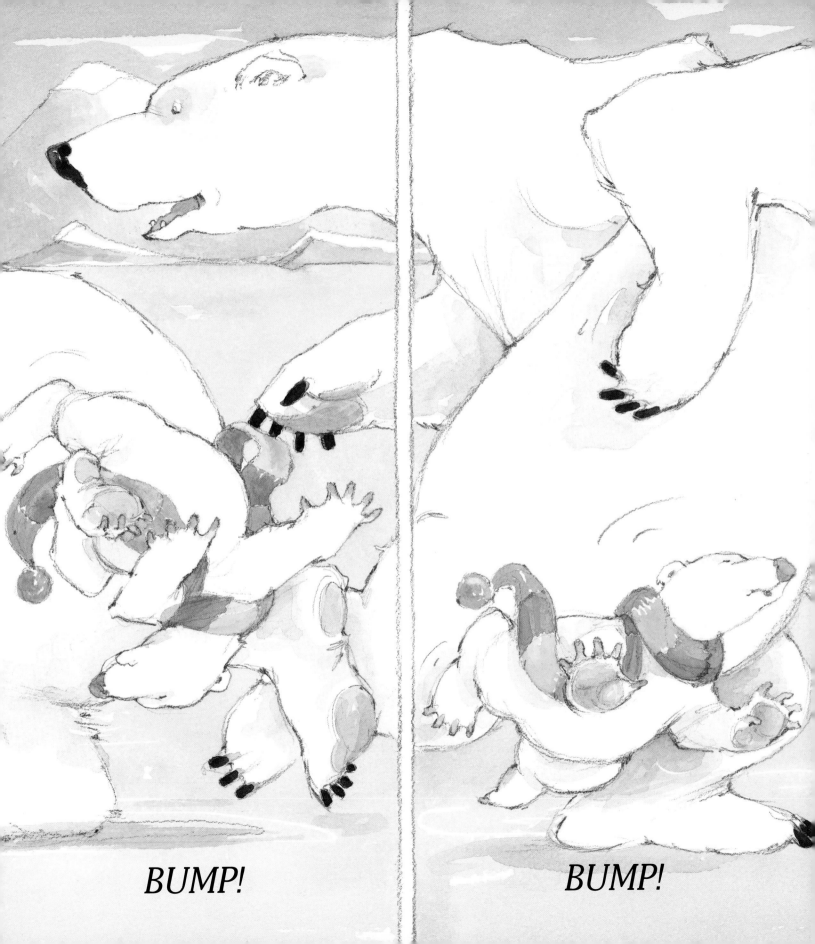

BUMP!   *BUMP!*

Little Mo started to cry and she turned away.
She didn't like the ice anymore.

"It was all *my* idea,"
Little Mo said to herself.

The Big Ones got tired and went home.

They forgot Little Mo.

Little Mo looked at the ice
and she liked it again.

She slid and. . .

she fell. *BUMP!*

She got up and then she
did it again without falling,

and again

and again   and again . . .

all by herself,
sliding around on the ice . . .

and Little Mo loved it.

MARTIN WADDELL is one of the most prolific and successful children's writers of his time, having written more than one hundred books for children, including *Can't You Sleep, Little Bear?*, *Farmer Duck*, *Owl Babies*, and *The Big Big Sea*. A former semiprofessional soccer player in England, he found that "when I played with my children, I became too enthusiastic and ended up spoiling their games."

JILL BARTON remembers behaving the same way herself as a parent—particularly when her family first bought the board game Clue. She is also the illustrator of *The Happy Hedgehog Band* and *The Pig in the Pond*.